PRANCER

written by
Stephen E. Cosgrove

◆

based on a screenplay by
Greg Taylor

◆

illustrated by
Carol Heyer

Graphic Arts Center Publishing Company
Portland, Oregon

International Standard Book Number 1-55868-009-8
Library of Congress Number 89-83843
Text © MCMLXXXIX by Nelson Films, Inc.
Illustrations © MCMLXXXIX by Graphic Arts Center Publishing Company
Published by Graphic Arts Center Publishing Company
P.O. Box 10306 • Portland, Oregon 97210 • 503/226-2402
Editor-in-Chief • Douglas A. Pfeiffer
Associate Editor • Jean Andrews
Designer • Becky Gyes
Typographer • Harrison Typesetting
Printer • Ringier America
Printed in the United States of America

Dedicated to those special dreams at Christmas time.
If you believe—and you must believe—
dreams can, and do, come true.
Stephen

ike crystal snows that swirled and blew, the Christmas spirit that year seemed to twist in circling eddies. Oh, there was spirit of a sort, but it seemed muffled in the wraps of patched woolen scarves and caps that needed replacing. Nowhere was this more evident than in the little farming town of Three Oaks.

The village decorations—holly wreaths and candy canes—were hung haphazard from the street lamps along the way. Christmas carols were being sung without conviction by school children as they followed their teacher from shop to shop. Even the Three Oaks pride and joy, the Santa display that annually stretched from one side of Main street to the other, this year sagged and creaked in the biting winter wind.

But there was one child in Three Oaks who bubbled over with spirit. Eight-year-old Jessica Riggs still believed in dreams and a jolly old elf called Santa Claus. She had every reason not to have spirit nor dreams: her mother had died nearly two years ago, and she lived alone with her father, who didn't seem to have time for any Christmas spirit.

One fateful day in December, as she was on her way home, the third reindeer in line on the display wibbled and wobbled in the wind, falling with a crash to the ground. Jessica rushed into the street and looked down at the broken reindeer where it lay. The white diamond patch on its forehead was smudged with a tire track, and one wooden leg was twisted and broken.

"Oh, dear," she said. "This was the third reindeer in line. That would be . . . let me see . . . 'On Dasher, on Dancer, on Prancer, on Vixen.' Oh, no! It's Prancer that fell. Whatever will Santa do with only seven reindeer?"

Her question went unanswered, and Jessica ran home to ask her father. "Daddy, daddy," she cried as she rushed into her father's barn, her cheeks winter-wind blushed by her run from town, "Prancer fell from Santa's sleigh. How will the reindeer pull the sleigh when there are only seven instead of eight?"

"Listen Jessica," chuckled her father, as he stacked old wooden crates, "It's time you learned that Santa Claus is nothing more than a bunch of silly nonsense. There is no Santa. Those reindeer are made of wood and paint. Dreams are for little children, and you are growing up. Now it's getting late. It's time to do your chores."

He laughingly turned back to his work, not noticing the tear that curved down Jessica's cheek. She turned and ran from the barn and up the hill toward Antler Ridge.

essica had always believed in dreams, and a part of those dreams at this time of the year was Santa Claus and the delightful Christmas spirit he brought. Now her father said that there was no Santa Claus and that dreams were silly. It was more than an eight-year-old could bear. With tears blurring her vision, she stumbled deep into the forest behind the barn.

Her crying was stopped, however, when the trees began to creak and groan as if blown by the wind. But the air was silent—still. Jessica looked around, for she sensed that she was being watched and followed. Her run slowed first to a walk, and finally she stopped.

"Who's there?" she shouted.

But the forest was still. No one answered. Maybe it wasn't a who. Maybe it was a what. Maybe it was a bear, or a lion, or a tiger.

But no monster leaped out from the forest. The woods became even quieter, muffled by the now-falling snow.

Finally, Jessica turned quickly around and there behind her wasn't a bear, a tiger, nor a lion. It was a tiny reindeer with soft velvet horns and big furry feet!

Curious, Jessica turned her head to the side, and, oddly enough, the reindeer did the same. She nodded her head, and the mischievous reindeer once again imitated her every move. She gently patted him on his rump and noticed two queer things: the reindeer was limping as if his front leg was injured, and he had a white diamond patch on his forehead.

"Oh, you poor, sweet thing," cried Jessica, as she looked at this strange little deer. Suddenly, her eyes opened wide in understanding, "Why, you must be one of Santa's reindeer. You . . . you must be Prancer!" As if to say "yes," the reindeer shook his head, and the crystal snowflakes danced about like magical confetti.

With the sun setting low, she led the limping reindeer down from the woods and into a rickety storage shed that stood behind the barn. The shed had no light, so Jessica looked around for a lamp or a candle. All she could find was a set of old-fashioned Christmas lights. She plugged them in, and the dingy shed twinkled in a rainbow of red, blue, green, and gold lights.

In the soft glow, she carefully bound the reindeer's injured leg with her scarf. Then with his leg bandaged, he hobbled about sniffing and "whoofing" at this and that, as Jessica wondered aloud what to do. "Santa Claus needs all of his reindeer to pull the sleigh. Without all of them, some toys won't be packed, and some children won't get a thing for Christmas. Somehow, we must let Santa know you're all right. Then he can pick you up on Christmas Eve."

Jessica paced about trying to come up with a plan. Finally, she snapped her fingers, nearly scaring the little reindeer out of his wits. "I've got it!" she cried, "I'll write Santa a letter."

She rushed to the house and, with an apple in hand, she skittered up the stairs to her room. She found paper and pencil and laid them carefully out on the braided rug. Then, with a snap as she bit into the juicy apple, she wrote:

> *Dear Santa,*
>
> *I found Prancer. He must have fallen. He hurt his leg, but I fixed it! He misses you and the other reindeer a whole bunch. I'll meet you two days before Christmas near midnight behind my house at Antler Ridge. Don't be late.*
>
> *Love,*
> *Your friend, Jessica*

She had just finished the apple and the letter, when her father popped his head in the door. Quickly, Jessica stuffed the letter into her back pants pocket.

"Jessie," he said, "I'm sorry I hurt your feelings earlier, but you just have to understand that Santa Claus is only for little tiny kids."

Jessica dropped her head as she guiltily felt the note in her pocket. She hated not telling her father the truth, but he just didn't believe.

he next day, right after school, she ran as fast as she could to the center of town. There, a Santa sat in a red velvet chair greeting children of all sorts, who had come to tell him what they wanted for Christmas. Jessica patiently waited her turn and then clambered up on his lap.

"I know you're not the real Santa Claus," she said in a hurried whisper, "and that you are just one of Santa's helpers. But I need your help to get a special letter to Santa." With that, she reached into her coat and withdrew her carefully written letter. "Tell him I have found Prancer and he can meet me tomorrow night at Antler Ridge."

The Santa sat back and chuckled a bit. "Ho, ho," he laughed, "and just how do you know this is Santa's reindeer?"

"Because," patiently sighed Jessica, "I saw Prancer fall from the display in town and he has the white diamond shape on his head." Satisfied now that all would be well, she jumped down from Santa's lap and ran home.

But Santa Claus was really no more than Mr. Young who ran the local newspaper. Later that evening back in his office, as he removed his Christmas trappings, Mr. Young found the letter Jessica had written to Santa Claus about how she had found Prancer and had taken care of his injury.

"Hmm," he mumbled, "this just might be a special story that will bring a little bit of Christmas spirit to all of the good folks who live in Three Oaks."

With that, he quickly went to work preparing the next day's paper. The presses clanked and groaned into the night, as the snow continued to fall.

Late the next afternoon, as the sun turned the silvered shadows of day to pinks and darker purples, Jessica sat in her bedroom and gazed longingly at Antler Ridge. "Tonight, tonight," she thought. "Tonight Prancer will be going home."

Her secret plans were rudely interrupted by the sound of people laughing and shouting from outside. There on the front lawn, illuminated by the rising full moon, was a crowd of people shouting, "Where's

Prancer?" Clutched in everyone's hands were copies of that evening's newspaper. The headlines read:

LITTLE GIRL FINDS PRANCER!

"Oh, no," cried Jessica as she pulled on her boots, "Father will be angry and, worse yet, Prancer may be in real danger."

Jessica slipped down the back stairs and, with her coat in hand, was out the kitchen door before anyone saw her. She whisked down the path, through the snow, to the shed where Prancer was hidden. With a screech-creak the door was opened and shut. She was safe with Santa's reindeer.

Prancer looked at her with trusting eyes as she knelt and removed the scarf wrapped around his leg. There, in the fading light of day and the trickling stream of bright moonlight, she found that the leg was amazingly healed. Almost like magic, the reindeer no longer limped.

Suddenly, the door burst open, and there stood her father.

"Jessica," he said, "I know what you are trying to do, but this old reindeer isn't Prancer. He probably just wandered away from a zoo, and now it's time we took him home. You take your time and say goodbye. I know that you'll do the right thing." And with that, he left the two of them alone.

Jessica waited a moment and carefully opened the shed door, looking at the yardful of people. What was the right thing to do? Should she believe in her father or in her dreams?

Resolved, she took a deep breath and ducked back inside. "Come on Prancer, we're going to have to run for it."

The door slammed open wide, and Jessica and the full-grown reindeer bolted from the shed and raced into the forest. The two of them ran through the orchard and up the hill toward Antler Ridge. In the distance, she could hear the pounding of feet and her father demanding that she stop.

On she raced, until she knew she could run no more. "Go on, Prancer," she panted. "You can run much faster than I. Go find Santa."

She turned and saw her father following their tracks up the hill. When she looked back, the reindeer was gone. "Oh, no!" she cried, "Prancer is gone and I didn't even get to say goodbye!"

Before she could chase after the reindeer, she was swept into her father's arms. "Jessica, Jessica," he said, hugging her tight.

"I didn't mean to disobey," she sobbed, "but you told me that you knew I would do what was right. And I did. Now I must follow Prancer because I didn't have a chance to say goodbye to him, and I didn't even get to see Santa."

"Listen," said her father gently, "Santa isn't real. And the reindeer you found couldn't be Prancer."

"But it really was Prancer," Jessica insisted, "and Santa is real! Come with me and I'll show you."

With that, Jessica slipped out of her father's arms and followed the fresh reindeer tracks in the snow. Her father sadly shook his head and trailed reluctantly along. Up and up they went, following the tracks until they came to the very edge of Antler Ridge.

Here, the tracks stopped in midstride, and here Jessica and her father stopped, afraid to look down for fear the reindeer had fallen to its death.

Tears streamed down Jessica's cheeks as her father reached down to comfort her. It was then, when all seemed lost, that a great tinkling of bells rang down on the earth like laughter laughed from afar. They both looked up, and there, silhouetted against the moon, was a sleigh pulled by not seven, but rather eight, tiny reindeer.

A gift was given that moonlit
night two days before Christmas, a gift that
would never be forgotten by those who had been
there, and by many who had not. The gift was
wrapped in silvered moonbeams. It was a wonderful
gift—the gift of believing in all sorts of dreams.

Other books in the DreamMaker Classic series: